Monster Maze

by

Douglas Hill

Illustrated by Tony Ross

You do not need to read this page - just get on with the book!

First published in Great Britain by Barrington Stoke Ltd
10 Belford Terrace, Edinburgh EH4 3DQ
Copyright © 2001 Douglas Hill
Illustrations © Tony Ross
The moral right of the author has been asserted in
accordance with the Copyright, Designs and
Patents Act 1988
ISBN 1-84299-006-3
Printed by Polestar AUP Aberdeen Ltd

MEET THE AUTHOR – DOUGLAS HILL

What is your favourite animal?
Cats - any and all
What is your favourite boy's name?
Michael - my son's name
What is your favourite girl's name?
Lauren
What is your favourite food?
Chocolate
What is your favourite music?
Mozart
What is your favourite hobby?
Reading

MEET THE ILLUSTRATOR – TONY ROSS

What is your favourite animal?
Cat
What is your favourite boy's name?
Bill
What is your favourite girl's name?
Roxanne
What is your favourite food?
Lobster
What is your favourite music?
Irish
What is your favourite hobby?
Sailing

For Declan and Eoin
who arrived on this planet
not so long ago

Contents

Chapter 1
Mystery World

"Dust and rock!" Perrin grumbled. "The first planet we find and it's all dust and rock!"

Perrin was in the control room of a starship. He was gazing out of a window-port at a nearby planet, which seemed to be stony, dusty and lifeless.

"At least we have *found* a planet," said Mirry, Perrin's friend, who was flying the

ship. "We might find something interesting when we scan it more closely."

The ship set off in a slow circle around the planet. Mirry switched on a scanner to get close-up pictures of the bleak, empty surface.

"There is something like air round this planet," Mirry announced. "But it is a gas that would be deadly to humans."

"Oh, wonderful," Perrin groaned.

"There are also a few patches of ice," Mirry added.

"Terrific," Perrin sighed.

Then Mirry twitched. "How strange," she said. "The scanner shows faint signs of *life*!"

"*Aliens*?" Perrin said. "Down *there*?" And he turned with an eager smile to look at the scanner screen.

Perrin was a young man, not very tall, with brown hair and a plain face. He had been in space, planet-finding with Mirry, for only three weeks. And he had spent nearly all of that time doing very little. Just watching TV, reading, playing computer games, gazing at the stars ...

But Perrin didn't mind. He liked a quiet life. Anyway, most of the work – flying the ship and so on – was done by his friend Mirry.

Mirry was small and neat, and also smooth and shiny – because she was a robot. On one of her shoulders the letters MIRI had been printed, which was the name of the company that built her. But when Perrin first met her he had thought it sounded like a girl's name. And since the little robot hadn't actually been given a name, Perrin called her Mirry, and thought of her as a girl robot.

In fact, Mirry was a *super*-robot. Her brain was more powerful than the Earth's biggest and best computer and her metal body was very strong and almost unbreakable.

Also, Mirry had been made for the job of planet-finding. So she was the one who had spotted the stony world, their first planet.

And she was about to spot a mystery on that world. As she and Perrin peered at the scanner, Mirry went very still. "That is *impossible*!" she gasped.

On the screen, a blue dot was flashing.

"That light," Mirry said, "shows that there is a life-form on the surface below. Only *one*, of a fair size, and it is *moving*. On a world where we have seen nothing that could support life!"

Chapter 2
Sudden Darkness

As Perrin peered at the blue dot, a loud chime sounded in the control room. His heart sank. That chime meant that they had a call from Earth, on the space-link. And Perrin knew who the call was from.

He turned towards the space-link screen, and saw the frowning face of a man. It was Commander Cragg, the head of the Planet-Finding Project, on Earth. And he was looking annoyed.

But then he almost always looked annoyed. The commander didn't think much of Perrin and hadn't wanted to give him the planet-finding job. It was Mirry who had insisted on having Perrin, because she liked him. After that, Cragg always expected Perrin to make a mess of things.

"Well, Perrin?" Commander Cragg barked. "Do you have anything useful to report, for once?"

"Yes," Perrin said stiffly. "We've found a planet!"

"It's about time," the commander growled. "You've been looking for three whole weeks ... I hope it isn't some useless dead lump of dirt."

Perrin gulped. "Why, um ... no," he said. "We're still scanning, but we know the planet has some sort of air. And it ... it's *full* of life!"

"Really?" the Commander said. "Excellent! Send a full report when you've finished scanning." And he switched off the space-link.

"Perrin!" Mirry sounded shocked. "You lied to him!"

Perrin squirmed. "Just a little fib," he mumbled. "Anyway, there *is* life on the planet."

"We have located only *one* life-form," Mirry reminded him. "The commander will be furious when he finds out."

"There might be more life, somewhere," Perrin muttered.

"That is not likely," Mirry said. "But at least the one life-form we have spotted has stopped moving. See, it is in the area just below us. So we can land and look for it."

"Do we have to?" Perrin groaned.

"Of course we do," Mirry said. "We must see what it is like."

With a sigh, Perrin turned to look out of the window-port. By then, they were hovering over a part of the planet's surface that was all broken and rugged. Perrin could see a vast network of deep, rocky gullies. They criss-crossed in wild confusion and stretched on and on into the distance ...

"The alien thing is down *there*?" Perrin asked. "Somewhere in all those gullies?"

"Ravines," Mirry said. "They are deeper than gullies."

Perrin shrugged. "It won't be easy to find it there. Look at how tangled the *ravines* are, the way they join up and cross and come to dead ends." He smiled. "It's like a giant maze. We should land in the middle and see if we can find our way out."

Mirry stared at him. "Why would we want to do that?"

"Mazes can be fun," Perrin told her. "It's sort of a game getting out of them."

"Robots do not play games," Mirry told him. "Besides, looking for a life-form on an alien world is a serious matter, Perrin."

The starship swooped down to land, in a ravine at the heart of the tangled maze. Quickly Perrin pulled on his light but tough space-suit. Then they opened the airlock and stepped out onto the landing ramp, into the alien sunlight.

Perrin flicked on the voice-link in his helmet, which connected him to Mirry. "Where's the life-form?"

"Somewhere near ..." Mirry began. Then she pointed. "Look, there!"

Perrin looked – and saw a flash of dark purple behind some rocks.

But then he could no longer see anything. Suddenly, the ravine had been plunged into total darkness.

Chapter 3
Impossible Terror

"Mirry!" Perrin gasped. "What's happened?"

"Back into the ship, Perrin," Mirry said quickly.

"It's as if something shut off the sun," Perrin mumbled, as they hurried back into the safety of the ship.

"That is unlikely," Mirry said. "But I cannot think what could have happened."

Back in the control room, they peered out at the blackness. Then Perrin jumped with new shock. The weird darkness suddenly vanished and the sun blazed brightly again.

Mirry looked at the scanner. "The alien life-form is running away, through the ravines."

"And I suppose we have to go after it," Perrin sighed.

"We must learn more about it," Mirry said, "and about this planet. It is our job. We may discover something useful, which would keep Commander Cragg from being too angry when he learns that you lied to him."

"It was just a fib," Perrin muttered, as they headed back to the airlock to start their search.

Outside, they set off along the ravine where the ship had landed. Before long they turned off into another ravine, which meant they could no longer see the ship.

Perrin looked around at the grim land. "I'd hate to get lost here."

"You said this was like a maze, and you said mazes were fun," Mirry reminded him.

Perrin shrugged. "They're not fun if they're dangerous."

"Quite true," Mirry agreed. "A maze you cannot escape from is a trap. But do not worry. I have a built-in link with our ship. I always know just where it is."

That made Perrin feel better, but he still kept peering around. After all, they were looking for an unknown creature. And they had no weapons.

The planet-finding rules said that alien life-forms were never to be harmed. Still, Perrin knew that his space-suit would protect him against many dangers. And so would Mirry with her robot strength. Her metal body was tougher than the thickest armour.

As they turned into another ravine, Perrin was wishing that they could have brought the scanner out of the ship, to help find the alien creature in that enormous maze. Mirry was studying the ground, looking for the creature's tracks. But Perrin couldn't see anything on the stony ground that looked like footprints.

Then they both jumped. Behind them, they heard a deep rumble like distant thunder. They spun round to see an enormous monster stamping towards them.

The monster seemed to be made of different bits that didn't fit. And all of them

were terrifying. It had the head, shaggy body and long arms of a giant ape. But its legs and tail were covered with the leathery, green skin of a crocodile. And on its head it had the long, curved horns of a mighty bull.

Perrin turned pale, but Mirry gazed calmly at the horror. "It may be an intelligent life-form, Perrin," she said. "It may speak to us."

Perrin's hand shook as he reached up to his helmet to switch on his Word-Wizard, a tiny super-computer that could work out a whole alien language from just a few words.

Mirry's robot mind could do the same thing, but there was a problem. The planet-finding rules said that first contact with any alien must be by a *human*. So it was Perrin who had to speak first.

But the weird-looking monster said nothing. Instead, it bared its giant fangs, bellowed like a bull and charged at them.

Chapter 4
Nightmare Creatures

"*Run!*" Perrin yelled.

He and Mirry set off at full speed. They couldn't head back towards their ship, because the towering monster was in the way. So they ran in the other direction, away from the ship, with the monster thundering after them.

After a moment, Perrin and Mirry swung into a side ravine, then dashed into another one, off to the right – then another and another ...

At last Mirry stopped. "Wait, Perrin!" she said. "It's no longer chasing us!"

Perrin listened, but all he could hear was his own puffing. There was not a sound from the monster.

"Maybe it's sneaking up on us," he said.

Mirry said nothing, as if she was lost in thought.

Then Perrin heard a new sound, from nearby. A scuttling sound.

"Mirry!" he gasped. "Did you hear that?"

Still Mirry said nothing. She stood still, and her eyes had gone dim.

Perrin groaned. Mirry did that, now and then. It was as if she somehow shut down, briefly, inside her mind, and stopped paying attention to things around her. But she would never *admit* that she did it.

"*Mirry*!" Perrin cried. "Switch back on! This is no time for one of your absent-minded moments!"

She twitched, and her eyes returned to normal. "I do not *have* absent-minded moments," she said firmly. "I was just thinking – about what a very strange creature that was ..."

"*Listen*!" Perrin yelled. "There's something *else* coming this way!"

Then, at last, Mirry too seemed to hear the scuttling sound.

And a moment later the creature that was making the sound surged into view.

It was as huge and horrible as the first monster. And it was also a crazy mixture of different creatures.

It had a massive, slithery body and stumpy legs, like a giant centipede. It also had long arms like an octopus *and* enormous pincer claws like a crab, *and* a curled-up tail like a scorpion with a huge, deadly sting.

Perrin stood frozen with shock, as Mirry studied the new horror. "I cannot understand how such a thing can exist," she said.

"We can worry about that later!" Perrin yelled. "Run!" They raced away as the monster hissed and charged in a scuttling rush.

Chapter 5
The Mystery Deepens

Perrin and Mirry headed towards the narrow opening of another side ravine. This one also led into another, and another, through more of the maze's twists and turns. But soon they stopped, when they could hear no more scuttling or hissing.

"That one's stopped chasing us too," Perrin said, puffing.

Mirry said nothing.

Perrin frowned. "Mirry, don't go absent-minded again."

"I do *not* go absent-minded," Mirry insisted.

"You always say that," Perrin replied. "But you *do*. You switch off. And one day it's going to get us into serious trouble."

"Nonsense," Mirry said sharply. "I just pause now and then to think about things. Which *you* might do more often, Perrin."

Perrin sighed. "All right. But it's not a good idea to stand around thinking when a big, scary monster is after us."

"It was the monsters that I was thinking about," Mirry replied. "It makes no sense that they are here at all, on this empty planet ... And why they are so different from one another ...?"

"And with horrible bits that don't belong together," Perrin added, "like something you'd see in a bad dream."

"Robots do not have dreams," Mirry said. "We do not sleep. But that is a good point, Perrin. The oddest thing is that all the different parts of the monsters look like oversized parts of *Earth* creatures. Apes, crocodiles, crabs, scorpions ... it is like a nightmare that a *human* might have."

"Then I want to wake up," Perrin muttered.

"Also," Mirry went on, "there is the mystery of the *first* creature we saw. The smaller, purple one that we glimpsed near the ship. I wonder what its link is with the other monsters ..."

She stopped – as they heard a deep, blood-freezing growl, from somewhere around the next corner.

"Not another monster!" Perrin gasped.

"I might try to *capture* this one," Mirry said calmly, "and take a close look at it."

Perrin twitched as he heard another growl, even closer. "Capture a huge, terrible monster?" he gasped. "It could tear you apart!"

"Not if I could *stun* it somehow from a distance ..." Mirry said.

But then the growling became a roar – and around the corner of the ravine a new nightmare appeared.

Not one monster this time, but *three* – looking partly like giant tigers, though covered in shiny scales instead of fur. But where the tigers' necks and heads should have been, the monsters had instead sprouted the upper bodies of *men*. They were huge and wild-looking, with ugly battleaxes and spiked clubs in their hands.

The sort of weapons used in olden times ... on Earth.

Chapter 6
Landslide

Perrin turned to run away. But Mirry stood still, gazing at the new horrors.

"Mirry, come on!" Perrin yelled. "You can't capture *three* of them!"

"You may be right," Mirry agreed. And they dashed away, with the tiger-men roaring after them.

Perrin's legs were soon wobbling, after so much running. So Mirry gripped his arm and almost carried him along with her robot strength. And soon, after they had dashed through many more ravines, they found once again that the monsters had stopped chasing them.

"That is another odd thing," Mirry said, as Perrin fought to catch his breath. "The monsters always give up so quickly."

"Just as well," Perrin panted. "Can we get back to the ship now?"

"We are a long way from the ship," Mirry told him. "First, we must try to find the answer to these puzzles. And you, Perrin, must find something to please Commander Cragg."

"I'll invite him to come and play with the monsters," Perrin muttered.

"Also, I still want to capture and study a monster," Mirry went on.

"Mirry, I want to go back to the ship," Perrin insisted. "I'm thirsty, hungry and worn out, and the air in my space-suit could run out soon ..."

"Not for hours," Mirry told him. "But we can start back towards the ship if you like."

So they set off again, at an easy pace, through the maze of stony and bleak ravines. And they saw no more signs of life.

"Most strange," Mirry said, as they moved into the shadows of a deeper ravine. "Huge monsters roaming around should leave some *traces*. But there is nothing."

"Maybe they don't roam in this part of the maze," Perrin said.

But at once he was proved wrong – by an ear-splitting *screech* from above.

Perrin looked up and saw six terrifying, flying creatures. They were the largest flying things he had ever seen, with powerful batwings like great, leathery sails. But instead of feathers or fur they were dripping with slime. And they each had four legs with massive claws, and two heads with hooked beaks like vultures.

"Run, Perrin!" Mirry said quickly. "I will try to knock one of them out of the air with a stone."

"A *stone*?" Perrin repeated, startled.

But Mirry leaped away, towards the cliff at one side of the ravine. Perrin saw that she didn't mean just any stone. She was reaching for a rock almost as big as herself, which was sticking out from the cliffside.

She gripped the big rock in her metal hands and jerked it free with inhuman strength. Then she spun to face the flying horrors.

But their screeches were drowned by a terrifying roar.

Somehow the rock had been holding up the side of the high cliff. When Mirry pulled the rock away, the cliff lost its support.

And the whole of it suddenly collapsed – in a thundering landslide of dust and gravel and huge rocks.

On top of Mirry.

Chapter 7
Alone and Lost

"Mirry!" Perrin yelled in horror, as the mass of rubble settled, blocking his way along the ravine. "*Mirry!*" he shrieked, as the flying monsters swooped down at him.

But his robot friend was buried under the landslide, and could not help him.

With a gasp and a sob, Perrin fled with the monsters screeching after him. Then he dodged into a side ravine – and another, and another ...

By then his lungs were on fire and his legs were shaking. Yet he kept going, through the maze of ravines. Soon he began to stumble and stagger, until at last he tripped on a stone and fell with a crash.

He wasn't hurt by the fall, thanks to his space-suit, but he was too tired to move. Then he discovered that the flying monsters had stopped chasing him. But as he lay there, gasping, he knew that he was still in deadly danger.

Without Mirry, he couldn't find his way back to the ship.

He was lost in that bleak, alien maze – and he had no hope of survival. He had no food or water, and before long he would have no air.

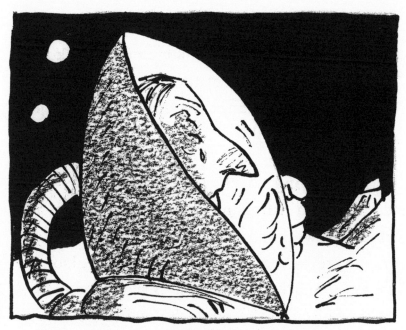

He closed his eyes to hold back tears of terror and despair. But then, after a while, he opened his eyes and got slowly to his feet.

I have to keep moving, he told himself. I might get lucky and stumble on the ship, before I run out of air. Or before another monster gets me ...

So he plodded on, helpless and hopeless.

As ever, each ravine led into another, and another, on and on. But Perrin took little notice. One bit of that dreary landscape looked much like another. And there was no sign of the starship.

Before long Perrin lost all sense of time. It felt like a different kind of nightmare, in which he walked endlessly and never got anywhere. And as he kept going, he also kept waiting for some new terror to appear. Or for the moment when he would no longer be able to breathe.

But then, as he turned into yet another ravine, he stopped. He had heard an unexpected sound. Not a terrible roar or screech – just a soft rattle, like a pebble rolling over other pebbles.

Something quiet and sneaky, he thought. Maybe that purple-coloured thing ...

For a moment he felt like just giving up. But then he told himself that he still had some air left in his space-suit, so he still had some chance. And he didn't feel like being torn to bits by an alien monster's claws.

He looked around and spotted a narrow crack in the wall of the cliff. Quickly he squeezed himself into the crack. Hidden in its darkness, he waited.

Soon he heard the rattle of stone upon stone again, but even closer. There was another sound too, a light thudding. As if something was trotting along the ravine.

Then the creature making the sounds came into view. And Perrin went stiff with surprise.

Chapter 8
Purple Intruder

"*Mirry*!" Perrin shrieked.

"There you are, Perrin," said the little robot. "I *thought* those must be your footprints."

Perrin was so amazed he could barely struggle out of the crack. Mirry's metal body didn't have a scratch on it, even though a ton of rocky rubble had fallen on it.

"I thought you were *crushed* under that landslide!" Perrin babbled.

"Not at all," Mirry said. "A few rocks cannot harm my metal." She tapped her shiny chest. "It just took me some time to dig myself out, before I could start following your tracks."

"Brilliant!" Perrin smiled. "I thought I was going to die here ..."

"In fact you have done very well, Perrin," Mirry said. "You have come a long way back towards the ship."

"Just luck," Perrin said. "I didn't know where I was."

"But now we must hurry to the ship," Mirry went on. "Before the last of your air runs out."

Perrin groaned. "I'm so tired – I don't

know if I *can* hurry ..."

"Never mind," Mirry said. "Get on my back, and I'll carry you."

So Perrin got on Mirry's back. And he was amazed again as she began to run – smoothly and at great speed – in spite of his weight.

"Did you see any more monsters?" Mirry asked, as they dashed along.

"No," Perrin said. "Did you?"

"Not one," Mirry said. "And still no traces of them, anywhere. They seem to disappear without leaving even a footprint."

"Like magic," Perrin muttered. "Maybe this planet is magical."

"Magic is not real," Mirry said. "But it could be something like it. I am still thinking about what you said, about the monsters being like things from a dream."

Perrin frowned. "But they can't be, really. *You* saw them – and you said robots don't have dreams."

"True," Mirry said. "But I believe ..."

She paused. They had come around a rocky corner that led from one ravine to another – and saw their starship, not far away.

But Perrin felt the chill of new fear as Mirry stopped and set him down.

A strange creature was standing on the ship's landing ramp. A *purple* creature, like the one they had glimpsed in the ravine, just after their arrival.

And it was trying to force open the airlock.

Chapter 9
Alien Threat

Mirry leaped towards the ship at inhuman speed. As Perrin followed, a lot more slowly, the alien saw them and scrambled wildly down the ramp.

But as the alien dashed away, Mirry was right behind it. The alien stopped and whirled around – and Mirry stopped too. When Perrin came up to them, they were standing still, staring at one another.

Perrin saw that the alien was wearing a purple space-suit with a clear helmet. It – he – was short, thin and more or less human-shaped, with grey skin, green hair and yellow eyes. And he was holding an alarming object in his hand.

It looked very much like a gun. And the alien was pointing it at Mirry.

But then the alien aimed the gun at Perrin. "*Eejee jeek deeb*!" the alien said.

Perrin jumped and switched on his helmet's Word-Wizard. "What?" he asked.

"*Deekeekeekee* ..." the alien began. And then the Word-Wizard started to translate the alien's words inside Perrin's helmet.

"Don't move!" the alien was saying. "Put down your weapons!"

"We don't have any weapons," Perrin gulped. And his Word-Wizard translated those words into the *alien's* language, through the speaker on Perrin's helmet.

The alien hesitated. "Well ... er ... just stay where you are!"

"W ... we come in peace ..." Perrin began, remembering the planet-finding rules.

"Be quiet!" the alien said, waving the gun. "Get back!"

"I haven't moved," Perrin pointed out.

"You'd better not!" the alien threatened.

"What do you want with us?" Perrin asked.

Again, the alien hesitated. "I don't want anything with you," he said at last.

He seemed to be shuffling his feet and hanging his head, as if he was *ashamed* about something. Perrin began to feel hopeful. But then the alien's next words filled him with terror.

"It's not you I want," the alien repeated. "I ... I want your *ship*."

Chapter 10
Strange Powers

"Our *ship*?" Perrin yelled, in near-panic. "You want to steal our *ship*?"

"I have no choice," the alien said, shuffling his feet. "My ship crashed on this planet. My link to my own world was broken. I've been *stuck* on this wretched empty planet for *ages*. Your ship is my chance to get away ..."

"Then *we'll* be stuck here!" Perrin yelled.

"Yes, well ..." the alien said. "Sorry."

"And do you also," Mirry asked, "have something to do with those monsters?"

The alien shrugged. "Never mind that," he said. "What I want you to do ..."

But Perrin had turned to Mirry. "Do you think he's in *control* of the monsters?"

"I said never *mind* that," the alien insisted.

"In a way," Mirry said to Perrin.

Perrin frowned. "Is that true?" he asked the alien. "Do you control the monsters?"

"Yes!" the alien shouted, and his yellow eyes blazed. "I have *mental powers*, understand? I made the darkness, first –

then I looked into your minds. There I found images of creatures from your world and used them to create those monsters!"

"To frighten us away?" Mirry said. "While you stole our ship?"

"Right!" the alien said. "And there's nothing you can do to stop me!"

"Do not be too sure," Mirry said flatly.

"No?" the alien snarled. "I'll show you!"

He pointed to the starship. At once, from behind the ship, another enormous, terrifying monster towered above them.

It was bigger than any of the others, and more horrible. It had the hairy body and legs of a giant spider, the spiky head of a mighty dragon, the deadly sting of a huge wasp, and the razor-sharp teeth of an enormous shark.

Yet Mirry stepped towards it, as if it didn't worry her at all.

At first Perrin cried out in horror – then he cried out in shock. Mirry had walked right *through* the monster, as if it was no more solid than air.

And the monster vanished.

Mirry nodded calmly. "As I thought," she said. "Monsters that leave no tracks or traces ... they are not *real*."

"How did you know?" Perrin gasped.

"You gave me the idea, Perrin," Mirry replied, "when you said that the monsters were like nightmares. I began to think that they might not be real. This alien cannot make real monsters. He was only making false images, *illusions*, to frighten us off."

"But why do all that, when he could simply have shot us?" Perrin asked. Then he frowned. "Unless that thing isn't really a gun ..."

"That is an interesting thought, Perrin," Mirry said.

"All *right*!" the alien yelled. "You think you're clever, but you still won't stop me! This thing may *not* be a gun, exactly. But it makes illusions by working on your minds – and it can also *blast* your minds! If you try anything, I'll turn you into a helpless idiot and a lump of useless metal!"

Chapter 11
Out of the Maze

Perrin took a step back. "Mirry!" he whispered. "He looks crazy enough to do what he says!"

"I'm warning you!" shouted the alien. "Open up this ship, and then back off, or I'll blast your minds!"

"No," Mirry said. "I do not believe you will."

And – just as she did with the dragon-monster – she stepped forward, towards the alien.

"Stop!" the alien shrieked. "Don't make me blast you!"

But Mirry kept coming and the alien didn't blast her. Instead, he backed away, and did nothing at all.

Mirry calmly reached out and took the weapon from his hand. "You have been telling lies," Mirry told him firmly. "This object is not any kind of *weapon* at all. As Perrin said – if it was, you wouldn't have had to use it to make the monsters. You could simply have blasted us."

The alien hung his head. "My people don't believe in harming other beings," he mumbled. "We invented this machine to keep our space explorers safe. It makes scary images that drive off dangerous alien creatures without hurting them ..."

"You're lucky *we* didn't have guns!" Perrin raged. "We might have blasted *you*!"

"I know," the alien mumbled. "I'm really sorry. But I was so *desperate* – I wasn't thinking – I couldn't bear to be stranded here any longer ..."

"All you had to do," Mirry said, "was to ask for help."

The alien nodded sadly. "I was afraid you'd say no and leave me here."

"That's what we *should* do," Perrin told him. "You were going to leave us."

"I planned to let you contact your world first," the alien said. "So they could send a ship to pick you up."

Perrin sniffed, "Do you think that makes it all right?"

"It makes it better," Mirry said. "And it must have been terrible for him, being stranded here."

The alien looked hopeful. "*Will* you help me, then?" he begged.

"Of course," Mirry told him. "We could not leave you. Could we, Perrin? He has said he is sorry."

Perrin sighed. "I suppose not."

"Oh, thank you, *thank* you," the alien babbled. "If you take me home, my people would make you ever so welcome. You'll *love* my world, it's so peaceful. My name is Jorj, by the way."

"I'm Perrin, and she's Mirry," Perrin said as they trooped into the ship. Then he looked at Mirry. "I wonder what Commander Cragg will say."

"I should think he will be delighted," Mirry said brightly. "And he will forget all about your *fib* about this planet. Because when we take Jorj home, we will have found a planet that really *is* full of life. A world of intelligent and peaceful aliens."

"Right," Perrin said. "Just the sort of thing we're supposed to be looking for." He laughed. "And a *whole* lot better than monsters!"

Barrington Stoke was a famous and much-loved story-teller. He travelled from village to village carrying a lantern to light his way. He arrived as it grew dark and when the young boys and girls of the village saw the glow of his lantern, they hurried to the central meeting place. They were full of excitement and expectation, for his stories were always wonderful.

Then Barrington Stoke set down his lantern. In the flickering light the listeners were enthralled by his tales of adventure, horror and mystery. He knew exactly what they liked best and he loved telling a good story. And another. And then another. When the lantern burned low and dawn was nearly breaking, he slipped away. He was gone by morning, only to appear the next day in some other village to tell the next story.

Barrington Stoke would like to thank all its readers for commenting on the manuscript before publication and in particular:

Andrew Beaney
Sarah Binyon
Kelly Bird
Amy Boe
Peter Carpenter
Christine Charlton
Jennifer Clarke
Harriet Curson
Angela Dominy
Michael Doran
Gareth Edwards
Jessica Foyle
Douglas Haggen
Kirsty Heber-Smith
Sophie Hewson
Tommie Introna
Alice Juckes
Lottie Kibble
Imogen Lane
William Langstone
Caroline Loven
Adeel Mahmood
Izzy Malik
Alexa Mannering

Tom Mawby
Fiona Moorcroft
Jason Nickerson
Max Paradise
Melissa Parkinson
Daniel Pitts
Steven Pitts
Anthony Portlock
Chris Poulter
Michael Prescott
Daniel Reid
Andrew Scott
Katie Shuttleworth
Ashleigh Simpson
Rebecca Sloan
George Smith
Joshua Studholme
Rianna Suen
Oliver Talbot
Adam Ward
Michael Wharton
Thomas Wicks
Alice Wilson

Barrington Stoke, 10 Belford Terrace, Edinburgh EH4 3DQ
Tel: 0131 315 4933 Fax: 0131 315 4934
E-mail: info@barringtonstoke.co.uk
Website: www.barringtonstoke.co.uk

If you loved this story, why don't you read ...

Starship Rescue

by Theresa Breslin

Who can save the Outsiders from a life of slavery? It is up to Marc and Sasha to get a message for help to Planet Earth. But as Marc discovers, not even friends can be trusted.

You can order this book directly from:
Macmillan Distribution Ltd, Brunel Road, Houndmills,
Basingstoke, Hampshire RG21 6XS
Tel: 01256 302699